The Good Night Knight

by Josh Will

There once was a knight that knighted at night.
He guarded the village from all sorts of fright.
Most thought he did so with muster and might.
But he harmed not a soul for that wouldn't be right.

Each night the villagers slept safe in their beds.
Each day they fed the Night Knight gravy and bread.
But he had too much food and was quite overfed.
Did he waste all that food? No! He saved it instead.

The knight was nice to the old village baker.
To the blacksmith, the barber and the bookmaker.
He smiled at everyone, even the undertaker.
The village trusted the knight, knowing he was no faker.

At sunset the knight made his way to the wall.
There he watched over the village, young, old, and all.
He protected them from the wild banshee's call.
From scissor-back sleaches and the dragon's sharp claw.

When the sun rose, the knight returned to the town.
Bringing back trophies for all that came 'round.
He had dragon scale dresses and cyclops's crowns.
Even wizard wind chimes making whizzing wind sounds.

One night the baker's son rose and snuck out.
He wanted to see what being a knight was about.
The boy climbed the wall and found a good place to scout.
But what he found there soon filled him with doubt.

Why, the good Night Knight was not slaying the beasts.
The knight wasn't harming them in the least.
Dragons and ogres their attacks weren't released
He was talking and trading and providing a feast.

The dragon gave him scales for gravy and bread.
The knight traded the ogre lemons for lead.
What happened at night was not what everyone said.
The Night Knight was friends with the things people dread.

The baker's son ran back into town.
He was very upset at what he had found.
He woke up the villagers and gathered them 'round.
He spoke of the knight's actions, which made them all frown.

Everyone in the village listened in awe.
What they had believed wasn't true at all.
The villagers had to see it so they went to the wall.
And what the boy had described is just what they saw.

The townspeople yelled at the knight angrily.
"Dear knight how could you befriend our true enemy?
You show these monsters much sympathy.
Now our town must prepare for a catastrophe!"

The knight turned to the people and calmly he said.
"Dear townspeople, my actions you have misread.
These creatures aren't foes, but are friends instead.
Let me explain how I keep you safe in your bed."

"They do not wish our people hate, hurt, or harm.
Seeking only food, they wish to trade with our farms.
Once you get to know them, they each have their charms.
So, you see, there's really no need for alarm."

"The ogres from the north enjoy citrus fruits.
Give a waffle to a wolf and you'll have brand new boots.
We can work out a deal for a flying frog flute.
There is no need to fight them. The point is quite moot."

The townspeople formed a line that was long.
They approached the knight who stood there so strong.
"We're sorry sir knight. You were right all along.
Can you ever forgive us? We see we were wrong."

The good knight smiled and patted the Baker boy's head.
The baker's son looked up with all his fears shed.
He offered the cyclops some warm fresh baked bread.
And the cyclops accepted with huge arms outspread.